MATT

The Second-Best Children in the World

MARY LAVIN

The Second-Best Children in the World

Illustrated by Edward Ardizzone

HOUGHTON MIFFLIN COMPANY BOSTON/1972

LIBRARY OF CONGRESS CATALOG CARD NUMBER 70-135132
ISBN 0-395-13896-5
PRINTED IN THE UNITED STATES OF AMERICA
FIRST PRINTING W

To

Kathleen MacMahon

and

Daniel and Hannah Ardizzone

When I was going around the world, I met three children going the other way.

The biggest was BEN.

He was TEN.

The second was **KATE.**

Kate was **EIGHT.**

The

OTHER

ONE

was

SO

small,

I could hardly see him at all.

It was a good thing he had his name on the band of his hat.

His name was MATT.

They told me that their FATHER and their MOTHER were the BEST father and mother in the world. When their father came home tired from work he always gave them piggy-back rides all over the house:

not only **UP** the stairs but

DOWN

—as well.

And every Sunday he took them on a TRIP.

Their mother was very kind, but she never had time to play. She had to stand all day long at the stove because she had so many meals to cook.

One day Kate spoke to Ben. "We have the BEST father and mother in the world," she said, "but they work too hard. They will get tired. And if they get tired, they will get cross. And if they get cross they will NOT be the best father and mother in the world any more."

"Do not worry," Ben said. "I have a PLAN. I will take you and Matt on a trip, and while we are away our father and mother can put their feet up. We will go on a long trip. We will go around the world."

"That is a good idea," Kate said. "Let us go and tell our mother and father."

When they told their father he was glad.
But their mother was worried.

"If you go on a long trip you will wear out the soles of your shoes," she said.

"Do not worry," Ben said.

"I HAVE A PLAN—

we will walk on our heels."

Then the children said goodbye to their mother and father and set off down the path to the road. Just as they reached the gate, their father got an idea. He called them back.

"If we are going to put our feet up while you are away, why don't we give you the car?"

"That is a VERY good idea," Ben said. "You are very kind. Thank you."

The children got into the car. Ben and Kate sat in the front; Matt had to sit in the back. They all waved to their father and mother and Matt leaned over and blew the horn. Then they drove off.

But the car was very old. It had not gone far before it STOPPED DEAD.

"Oh dear," Kate said, "what will we do now?"

"Do not worry," Ben said. "I will think of a PLAN but first we must do a

KIND DEED.

In winter when the poor birds die of cold and fall down out of the sky we do not leave them lying on the hard ground. We dig a grave for them and cover them with leaves. We must dig a grave for our poor car."

So they got out, and dug a

BIG HOLE.

Just then an old man came along.
"What are you doing?" he asked.

When they told him, he was pleased.
"You are very kind children," he said.
"Some children are very cruel to their cars.
Come with me and I will give you a new one. I have lots and lots of cars. You can
TAKE YOUR PICK."

The children picked a BIG car, so they could ALL sit on the front seat. Then they thanked the old man, and they got into their car.

They waved.

Matt blew the horn.

And they drove off.

They drove all day long and when it got dark they climbed into the back seat and went to sleep.

The next day they drove off again.

They had not gone far before

SUDDENLY

they came to an

OCEAN.

"Oh dear," said Kate. "What will we do now?"
"Do not worry," said Ben.

"I HAVE A PLAN."

Beside the ocean there was a pier.
Tied to the pier there was a tug.

The captain of the tug was sitting on deck.
"Please, sir," Ben said. "Will you take us across the ocean?"

"No. I will NOT,"

the captain said. "Your car is too BIG.
It might sink my tug, and I cannot SWIM."

"Do not worry," said Ben. "I have a

PLAN.

WE can swim. You lend us your tug and while we are away you can

PUT YOUR FEET UP."

"That is a good idea," the captain said. "I need a rest." And he took up his sea-chest and went ashore.

"Thank you, sir," said Ben, and he went on board. But Kate was worried.

"Oh dear," she said. "I am afraid our car will not fit on the deck."

"Do not worry," said Ben. "I have A PLAN."

Ben piled the lifeboats on top of each other in the bow. Then he pushed the funnel down to the stern.

"Now there is plenty of room for the car," he said, "and the ship will be steady on top of the waves if we meet a storm at sea."

"I see you are a good sailor, my boy," said the captain. He put down his sea-chest and sat on it, and he put his feet up on a bollard.

"Thank you, sir," Ben said again.

Then Kate and Matt came on board, and Ben went below and started up the engine. When Ben came back on deck they all waved to the captain. Matt blew the siren. And they put out to sea.

Whenever there was a fog they blew the fog-horn, and whenever another ship got in the way they blew the siren. And every time they sighted land they put in to port and took their car for a drive.

Soon they had been to every place in the world.

Some places were hot.
Some places were cold.
Some places had so much grass.
And some places had so much sand.

And some places had so much ice and snow they had to get out of the car and push it from behind.

But they NEVER, NEVER

forgot to walk on their heels.

No matter where they went their shoes were

always NICE and SHINY.

But one day an AWFUL thing happened.

Their shoes began to get too small for them.
Then their clothes began to get too small.
And at last Matt's hat got SO small
you could not read the name on the band.

"Perhaps it is time we went back?" Kate said. "We have seen every place in the world."

"We haven't seen ROME," Ben said.
"And Rome is the best place of all."

'Oh no," said Matt. "Oh no.

The best place of all is

HOME."

"You are right, Matt," Ben said. "Let us go home."

So they sailed back to the pier where the captain had lent them his tug. Before Ben handed it over, he put everything back

THE WAY IT WAS

when they got it.

They thanked the captain for lending them the tug.

They got into their car.

They waved.

Matt blew the horn.

And they started off for home.
This time they drove

VERY FAST

and soon they came to their house.

"Oh dear," Kate said. "We forgot to buy a present for our father and our mother."

"Do not worry," said Ben.

"I HAVE A PLAN—

we will make a package of our car and give it to them."

So they jumped out of the car and they found PAPER

and STRING

and they made a big package of the car.

Then Ben made a hole in the paper

and Matt put in his hand and blew the horn.

Their father and mother came running out.

“Did you have a good rest?” Ben asked them.

“Yes, thank you,” their father replied.

“We have brought you a present,” Ben said, and then he handed them the package. When their father and mother opened the package and saw what was in it, they were very pleased.

"You must be the

BEST

CHILDREN

IN THE

WORLD,"

they said.

"Oh no," said Ben. "We are not the best.

We are only the

SECOND-BEST.

If we said we were the best we would be

STUCK-UP.

like this.

The BEST children ALWAYS

say they are only the

SECOND-BEST."

BUT

I think they were the

BEST.

WHAT DO YOU THINK?